Charlotte the Baby Princess Fairy was originally published
as a Rainbow Magic special. This version has
been specially adapted for developing readers
in conjunction with a Reading Consultant.

Special thanks to
Rachel Elliot
and Sarah Levison

Reading Consultant: Prue Goodwin, lecturer in literacy and children's books.

ORCHARD BOOKS

This story first published in Great Britain in 2015 by Orchard Books
This edition published in 2019 by The Watts Publishing Group

1 3 5 7 9 10 8 6 4 2

© 2019 Rainbow Magic Limited.
© 2019 HIT Entertainment Limited.
Illustrations © Orchard Books 2019

HiT entertainment

A CIP catalogue record for this book is available from the British Library.

ISBN 978 1 40835 449 0

Printed in China

MIX
Paper from
responsible sources
FSC® C104740
www.fsc.org

The paper and board used in this book are made from wood from responsible sources

Orchard Books
An imprint of Hachette Children's Group
Part of The Watts Publishing Group Limited
Carmelite House, 50 Victoria Embankment, London EC4Y 0DZ

An Hachette UK Company
www.hachette.co.uk
www.hachettechildrens.co.uk

Charlotte
the Baby Princess Fairy

Daisy Meadows

ORCHARD

www.rainbowmagicbooks.co.uk

The Fairyland Palace

Nursery

Emily's House

Rachel's House

Tippington Town

Story One

The Adventure Begins!

A New Baby Girl

Rachel Walker smiled as she held baby Jessica. "She's so sweet!" said Rachel.

"Look at her tiny fingernails," whispered Rachel's best friend, Kirsty Tate.

Mrs Walker, Rachel and Kirsty had come to visit Mrs

Walker's friend Emily and meet baby Jessica.

Suddenly Emily gave a huge yawn. "I'm sorry, I don't mean to be rude," she said. "I'm just so tired! Jessica was awake a lot last night."

"Why does she wake up in the night?" asked Rachel.

"All young babies wake up in the night to drink milk," explained Emily. "But for some reason she wouldn't go back to sleep again. It's not like her!"

Soon they said goodbye to Emily and Jessica and started walking back to Rachel's house. "I hope Jessica sleeps better tonight," said Mrs Walker. "Rachel, when you were a baby I used to wish I knew a magic spell to make you sleep!"

Rachel and Kirsty exchanged a smile. Their fairy friends would probably know a helpful spell or two! The girls

were great friends with the
Rainbow Magic fairies. They
had visited Fairyland and had
many magical adventures.

When they were home the
best friends ran upstairs and
into Rachel's bedroom. The
girls bounced on their beds and
smiled at each other.

"I'm so pleased you're here for the weekend!" said Rachel. "What shall we do this afternoon?"

But Kirsty was pointing at Rachel's dolls' house.

"I didn't know that your dolls' house had real lights," she said.

"It doesn't," said Rachel in surprise.

"But there's a light on," said Kirsty. "Look!" She pointed at the highest window. Something was glimmering inside. What could it be?

Chapter Two

Mini Magic!

"The light seems to be coming from the nursery," said Rachel. The girls knelt in front of the dolls' house and peeped in through the window.

The little nursery was filled with a gentle, warm glow.

There were pictures on the walls and a mobile hanging from the ceiling. And in the middle of the room, a tiny fairy stood next to a crib! She smiled at the girls.

"Hello," she said in a tinkling voice. "I'm Charlotte the Baby Princess Fairy. Would you like to come in?"

"Yes, please!" cried Kirsty and Rachel.

"Knock on the front door and close your eyes," said Charlotte.

Rachel tapped on the door. Then both girls closed their eyes. They felt the air whoosh around them. When they opened their eyes they saw they were fairies, with silky wings on their backs!

The girls stepped into the dolls' house.

The floor of the hallway was made of real wood, and the walls were decorated with pretty wallpaper. Charlotte came over and gave both girls a hug. She was wearing a beautiful flowery dress and had curly brown hair.

"I'm really happy to meet you," said Rachel. "But what are you doing in my dolls' house?"

Charlotte led them into the sitting room and they sat on the tiny doll sofas.

"My job is to make sure that all baby princesses are happy and sleep well," Charlotte explained. "I have a very special magical object to help me. My magical soft lion toy always lies in the crib of the newest baby princess in Fairyland. But last night, Jack Frost crept into the Fairyland Royal Nursery and stole the toy!"

Chapter Three

The Missing Lion

"Oh no!" cried Kirsty. "That's terrible. Jack Frost is so mean!"

Charlotte nodded, tears shining in her eyes. "When my toy is missing, baby princesses are the first to be unable to sleep, then the magic affects baby princes' sleep, and then non-royal babies. I'm sad to say that all fairy babies have had a terrible night. And now the missing magic toy has started to affect one or two human babies with a special connection to Fairyland."

"That must be the reason Jessica cried so much last night," said Rachel, and Kirsty nodded.

"Will you come with me to Fairyland?" Charlotte asked. "I really need your help to get my special toy lion back!"

"Of course we'll help you," said Kirsty, jumping up. "We won't let Jack Frost make those poor babies cry for another night!"

Charlotte fluttered to her feet and waved her wand. Magical sparkles swirled around them. The girls found themselves sitting on a fluffy white cloud, floating above the pink turrets

of the Fairyland Palace.

"I want to show you something," Charlotte said, looking serious.

The cloud swooped down and hovered beside a toadstool house. Through the window of the house the friends could see that a fairy mother and father were bending over a crib, where a tiny fairy baby lay crying.

"What's wrong, little one?" the fairy mother said. But the baby just kept crying.

Charlotte took Rachel and Kirsty all around Fairyland, swooping on the cloud through the night sky. They kept seeing the same thing: tired fairy babies everywhere!

"I want to help them, but I don't know how," said Charlotte.

"We will help you," said Rachel. "We'll stop Jack Frost!"

"The first thing we have to

do is fly to the Ice Castle," said Kirsty. "We need to find out what Jack Frost has done with the toy lion."

Hand in hand, Rachel, Kirsty and Charlotte left the cloud and bravely zoomed towards Jack Frost's Ice Castle.

Story Two

Jack Frost's Kingdom

Chapter One

The Goblin Village

Jack Frost's spooky castle looked very unwelcoming. Everything was dark and there were no goblins to be seen!

"There's a sign on the door," said Rachel, pointing down to the grand entrance. "Let's go and read it."

When the friends got closer they saw that the sign said 'Closed for Repairs'.

"Where would Jack Frost stay if he's not at his castle?" wondered Kirsty. "He doesn't have any friends to stay with!"

"I've only ever seen him with the goblins," said Charlotte.

"That's it!" cried Rachel.

"I'm sure he's staying in the goblin village."

The girls had visited the goblin village before. They headed down the winding, icy path towards the group of huts.

"Listen," said Kirsty as they got closer.

There was a lot of noise coming from the village. Giggles and gurgles filled the air!

"That sounds like a lot of happy babies," said Charlotte.

Rachel spotted a hut with a

sign outside the door. "'Green Goblin Nursery'," she read out, peeping through the window. Inside, she could see some goblin babies sitting up in a green playpen. They looked wide awake. A few of the babies were shaking Jack Frost-shaped rattles, and some were giggling and playing with each other.

A female goblin was fast asleep in an armchair, snoring so loudly that the plates on the table beside her were rattling.

"Look at this," Rachel said, as Kirsty and Charlotte joined her at the window. "It seems the goblin babies are finding it hard to sleep, too!"

Kirsty and Charlotte peered through the window.

"We should disguise ourselves," said Kirsty. "Goblins don't like fairies and they might be cross if they spot us."

"We really don't like fairies!" said a mean voice.

The three fairies spun around and gasped. There stood a group of angry goblins!

Chapter Two

Prisoners

One of the goblins reached forward and snatched Charlotte's wand out of her hand. The other goblins grabbed the fairies and pushed them into the hut opposite.

"Let us go!" cried Rachel.

But the biggest goblin closed
the door. It shut with a bang,
and the key turned in the lock.

The three fairies stared at each
other, feeling helpless.

"How can we get out of a locked room?" asked Charlotte with a groan. "I need my wand!"

"There are some keys hanging on the wall up there," said Kirsty. "Perhaps one of them will fit the lock."

She tried all of the keys, but none worked.

Rachel was thinking hard. "I have an idea," she said.

"Goblins aren't very clever, so if we can get a goblin to open this door, perhaps we can trick him into letting us out?"

Kirsty and Charlotte agreed this was a great idea. The three fairies made as much noise as they could. Rachel and Kirsty banged pots and pans together, and Charlotte hit the door with a walking stick she had found in a cupboard! At last they heard a goblin's voice outside the door.

"What's all this noise?" he grumbled crossly.

"We thought you should know that there are some door keys inside this hut," said Kirsty politely. "If you don't want us to escape, you'd better come and take the keys away."

There was a pause, and then the fairies heard the sound of keys

rattling. Moments later the goblin opened the door and

walked into the hut. Right away, Charlotte slipped behind him and blocked the doorway.

"What's going on?" the goblin shouted. He stumbled and tripped over his own large feet. He landed on his big bottom with a thud!

"Quick, let's stop him from getting up!" Rachel cried. She and Kirsty darted forwards and sat on his legs to stop him from running away.

Charlotte fluttered forwards and stood in front of him.

"We want to know if Jack Frost is here," she said. "He has something that belongs to me, and I want it back!"

Chapter Three

Charlotte's Promise

"I'm not telling you anything!" squawked the goblin. "Get off my legs!"

"We're not moving until you answer Charlotte's question," said Rachel.

"Is Jack Frost here?" Kirsty asked.

The goblin sighed loudly. Then he nodded his head. "He's staying in the goblin village until a leak in the Ice Castle is repaired," he said, sounding very grumpy.

"Don't you like having Jack Frost to stay?" Rachel asked.

The goblin folded his arms. "All he does is moan," he said. "He wrote a list of all the things that are wrong. Look!"

The goblin pulled out a piece of paper and showed it to the fairy friends.

My Complaints by Jack Frost

1. Bed is too lumpy. I am bruised all over.

2. Food is unpleasant. Sandwiches are not supposed to be green.

3. Ceiling is too low. I have bumped my handsome head too many times.

4. Goblin babies cry too much.

Rachel and Kirsty giggled. Clearly Jack Frost wasn't having a very nice time!

"He even brought a special toy to make the goblin babies sleep," the goblin went on. "But it hasn't worked. The babies haven't slept at all!"

Rachel and Kirsty raced over to Charlotte.

"Do you think Jack Frost has your special lion toy?" whispered Rachel.

Charlotte nodded, her eyes sparkling.

"But then why hasn't it helped the goblin babies to sleep?" asked Kirsty.

"The lion's magic is meant for fairy and human babies," said Charlotte. "Goblin babies are very different creatures!"

"The goblins must be very fed up," said Rachel. "I bet they wish they had a magical toy that worked on their babies' sleep."

"That's it!" said Charlotte. She turned back to the goblin. "If you show us where Jack Frost is, I promise I will make a special magical toy to help the baby goblins sleep."

"Will you help us?" Kirsty asked.

The goblin looked confused. "Goblins don't normally help fairies," he said.

"But it will make life much nicer if everyone can get a

good night's sleep," said Rachel.

The three friends looked at each other. Would the goblin agree to their plan?

Story Three

The Magical Lion

Chapter One

Irritable Ice Lord

The goblin nodded and jumped up. "OK, I'll help you," he said. "Follow me!" And he ran out through the door.

Rachel, Kirsty and Charlotte flew after him. As he led them through winding streets and past rickety huts, all they could hear were gurgles of baby goblin laughter!

"All the goblin babies still seem to be awake and playing," said Charlotte.

The goblin finally stopped outside a hut with a sign on the door saying 'Guests'. He took a deep breath and knocked on the door.

"Clear off!" barked an angry voice from inside the hut.

The friends recognised that voice … it was Jack Frost!

Rachel bravely opened the door of the hut and stepped inside. Kirsty and Charlotte followed, with the goblin hiding behind them.

There was a bed against the far wall of the hut, and there was a big lump in the middle of the bed. Kirsty stepped forward and pulled the covers back. Jack Frost was hunched over with his bottom sticking up in the air and his hands over his ears. A soft lion toy was tucked under his arm.

"That's my magical lion!" cried Charlotte.

Rachel and Kirsty stepped forwards and tapped Jack Frost on the shoulder.

"GO AWAY!" Jack Frost yelled, jumping up. He had dark shadows under his eyes, and his hair looked floppy. "All I want is a good night's sleep!"

"But it's the middle of the day," said Charlotte.

"Go away, you horrible fairies!" Jack Frost shouted angrily.

He snatched his wand up from a side table and sent a blue lightning bolt zooming across the room. Rachel and Kirsty dived out of the way of Jack Frost's magic.

Kirsty stood up. "We just want to talk to you about the lion—"

"I'm not talking to silly fairies about anything!" Jack Frost roared.

Another lightning bolt shot out of his wand. The three friends and the goblin raced outside and slammed the door closed.

"Well, we know where Jack Frost is!" said Kirsty. "Now we just have to work out how to get the magical lion toy back."

Chapter Two

Team Tactics

"You promised that you'd make a special toy to help the baby goblins go to sleep," yawned the goblin.

"I can't make the toy until I have my magic wand back," explained Charlotte.

"If you fetch Charlotte's wand, she can keep her promise," Rachel added.

The goblin ran off. Kirsty turned to the door of the hut.

"Jack Frost, listen to us!" she called through the door. "I know you're tired, and that's why you took Charlotte's lion

toy. But its magic doesn't work for goblin babies. That's why they're not sleeping."

"You're just trying to trick me!" Jack Frost shouted back.

Rachel spoke next, in a loud, clear voice.

"Charlotte has promised to make a special toy that will help the goblin babies to sleep," she said. "But she will only make the toy if you return the lion to her. You know that fairies always keep their promises!"

There was a long pause. Then the door handle turned, and the door opened a little. The fairies moved closer together. What was Jack Frost going to do?

"Here," the Ice Lord said in a sulky voice. "Take it. Just make those noisy babies go to sleep."

The lion toy was pushed through the door, and Charlotte hugged it to her.

Then the goblin ran up to them with Charlotte's wand clutched in his hand. Charlotte took the wand, and thanked the goblin. "Now for a little baby magic!" she said.

She raised her wand and sparkles swirled from its tip as she said some magical words:

"Goblin mums and dads must rest,
So sleeping babies would be best.
My soft toy will close their eyes,
And give one and all a peaceful night!"

The sparkles turned green and formed a fluffy frog toy. The frog dropped into Charlotte's waiting hands, and she passed it to the goblin.

"Go and give this to the youngest baby," she said.

He took it and darted off again. A few minutes passed and the fairies waited in silence. Rachel and Kirsty crossed their fingers. Would Charlotte's magic work on the baby goblins … ?

Chapter Three

And So to Sleep ...

A few moments later, all the goblin baby noises had stopped. All was silent until loud rumbling snores echoed from Jack Frost's hut!

"Time for us to go!" said

Charlotte with a smile. She waved her wand, and the friends were surrounded by a flurry of fairy dust.

They found themselves standing in a beautiful nursery. A snow-white crib stood in the middle of the room. The baby princess was still crying.

"Here's your special toy, sweet princess," whispered Charlotte, slipping the lion toy in beside the baby.

Right away the baby princess stopped crying and smiled.

She snuggled up against the toy lion and in a few seconds she was fast asleep.

Smiling, Charlotte tiptoed over to the window and gazed out over the pretty toadstool roofs and leafy forests of Fairyland.

"All the other babies in Fairyland and the human world will now be catching up on their sleep," she said with a happy sigh. "And it's all thanks to you!"

The three friends shared a

huge hug. "We're just happy that we were able to help," said Kirsty.

"We'll always help our fairy friends," Rachel added.

"Thank you from me and babies everywhere!" smiled Charlotte.

She lifted her wand and the nursery faded. The girls were back in Rachel's bedroom, kneeling in front of her dolls' house.

"What an adventure!" said Kirsty in delight.

Before Rachel could reply, the bedroom door opened and Mrs Walker came in. She looked very happy.

"Emily just called," she said. "Baby Jessica is now asleep, and that means that Emily can

catch up on her sleep too. Isn't that wonderful news?"

"It's the best news," said Rachel.

She and Kirsty smiled at each other. They knew why Jessica was sleeping so peacefully!

"Jessica must be a very special baby," Kirsty whispered as Mrs Walker left the room. "Perhaps one day, she will be a friend of the fairies too!"

The End

**If you enjoyed this story,
you may want to read**

Alyssa the
Snow Queen Fairy
Early Reader

Here's how the story begins …

"What a grey day!" said Rachel Walker, looking up at the dark clouds in the sky.

It was a Saturday morning in December, and Rachel was in her garden with her best friend Kirsty Tate.

"Ooh, it's starting to snow," smiled Kirsty. "But there's only one snowflake …"

A single, perfect snowflake drifted towards them. It began to grow bigger and bigger! Suddenly it burst and a tiny fairy appeared. She was wearing a long blue gown, decorated with sparkling sequins. A tiara twinkled on her head.

"Hello, Rachel and Kirsty," said the fairy. "I'm Alyssa the Snow Queen Fairy."

"Hello, Alyssa!" cried the girls.

"What are you doing here in Tippington?" Kirsty asked.

"I've come to ask for your help," said Alyssa. "It's my job to make sure that everyone stays happy in winter. But Jack Frost has taken my three magical objects. Without them, I can't look after human beings or fairies this winter."

"That's awful!" Rachel exclaimed. "How can we help you?"

"Please can you come to Fairyland with me?" Alyssa

asked the girls.

The friends nodded. "Of course we will," Kirsty replied.

Alyssa waved her wand and Rachel and Kirsty shrank to fairy size. How they loved being fairies! Rachel and Kirsty were good friends with the Rainbow Magic fairies and they adored the magical adventures they shared. The girls knew that time would stand still in the human world whilst they were away.

Moments later the girls were standing beside a tall white

tower. All around them were snow-topped mountains.

"Welcome to my home," said Alyssa, smiling at the girls. The friends went into the tower. It was warm and welcoming.

Alyssa explained how her magical objects had gone missing. "I went to visit Queen Titania this morning. When I came back my three objects were gone and there were goblin footprints in the snow!"

"What do your magical objects do?" Kirsty asked.

"The magical snowflake makes winter weather just right," Alyssa said. "The enchanted mirror helps everyone to see the difference between good and bad. And the everlasting rose ensures that flowers will appear again each spring. Without my magical objects, winter will be truly miserable for everyone!"

Alyssa and the girls decided to go to Jack Frost's castle and find the magical snowflake. As they flew through the grey skies of Fairyland, Rachel and Kirsty noticed the snow was icy and streaked with mud.

"This is happening because my magical snowflake is missing," Alyssa said. "It makes wintry weather enjoyable and I share that magic across the human and fairy worlds. With my snowflake missing, Fairyland and the human world will have nothing but grey skies and muddy snow. But Jack Frost will enjoy wonderful wintry weather!"

Sure enough, when they

reached the Ice Castle, soft
snowflakes were falling.

"Look!" said Rachel, pointing
to the castle gardens. Jack
Frost was reading to a group
of goblins. Beside him was a
table, and on the table was a
glass case. Inside the case was a
sparkling snowflake.

Read
Alyssa the Snow Queen Fairy
Early Reader
to find out
what happens next!

Meet the first
Rainbow Magic fairies

Can you find one with your name?
There's a fairy book for everyone at
www.rainbowmagicbooks.co.uk

Let the magic begin!

Become a
Rainbow Magic
fairy friend and be the first to
see sneak peeks of new books.

There are lots of special offers and exclusive
competitions to win sparkly
Rainbow Magic prizes.

Sign up today at
www.rainbowmagicbooks.co.uk